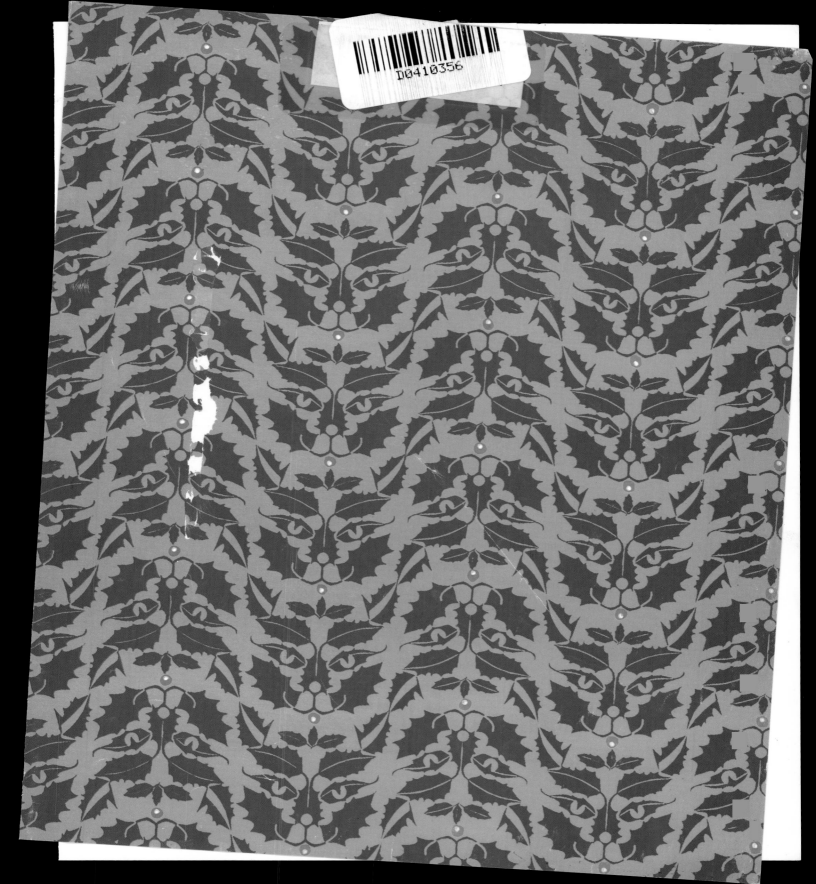

Dear Reader,

Fourteen years ago, on a cold November day, someone found a tiny, abandoned kitten. By coincidence they took her to our local vet, who knew that we wanted a kitten. Our dear old cat, Flossie, had died and the house seemed very empty without her. So we were delighted to welcome this small, homeless creature into our lives.

She was scraggy and thin and very nervous, but gradually she got used to us and settled into her new home. As she became more confident, she spent long, happy days investigating and exploring her exciting new world. But sometimes she would sit quite still, thinking deep thoughts.

When she was completely grown, she had two kittens of her own – a big boy and a tiny girl. We called them Buddy and Baby. She looked after them really well when they were little, but when they too were grown up she got rather bored with them. She always tried to sneak off on her own for some peace and quiet, but the other two usually found her.

She is an old lady now but she is still the boss. She is also still quick enough to catch me "presents". In fact, she brought me one this morning – I think she knew it was my birthday. Often she turns her back on the world and ignores everybody. Yet, every afternoon when I am working, she still comes and sits on my desk and keeps me company for a while.

So, this book is about her, and how she grew from being a tiny, frightened kitten into our big, beautiful and beloved Holly.

Ruth Brown
20th May, 1999

She was just a tiny kitten and she was abandoned.

Someone found her

and gave her to us.

Because it was nearly Christmas

we called her Holly.

She was timid Holly, at first...

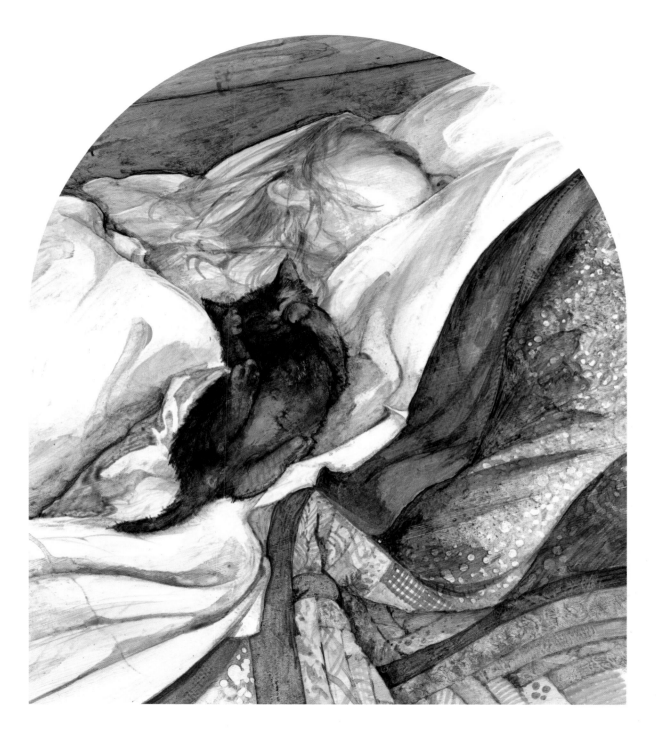

but as she grew she became relaxed Holly

inquisitive Holly

acrobatic Holly

adventurous Holly

fearless Holly

intelligent Holly

silly Holly

proud Holly

bored Holly

nosy Holly

exhausted Holly

bossy Holly

generous Holly

grumpy Holly

affectionate Holly

big, beautiful,

beloved Holly.

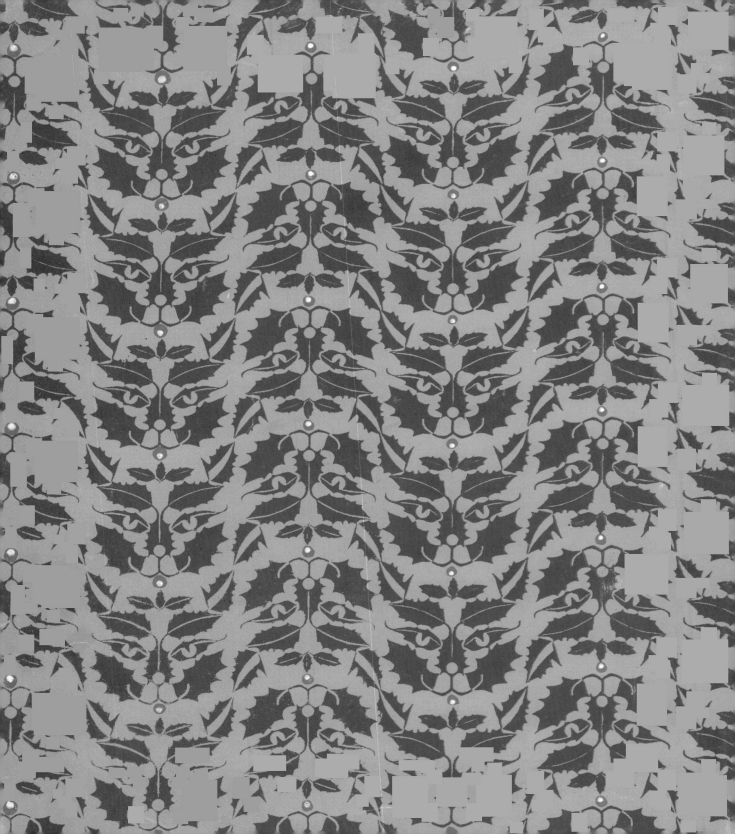